RICKS

Linda Chapman lives in Leicestershire with
her family and two Bernese mountain dogs.
When she is not writing she spends her time
looking after her two young daughters,
horse riding and teaching drama.

Not Quite a Mermaid

Mermaid

MERMAID TRICKS

LINDA CHAPMAN

Illustrated by Dawn Apperley

PUFFIN

PUFFIN BOOKS

Published by the Penguin Group
Penguin Books Ltd, 80 Strand, London WC2R 0RL, England
Penguin Group (USA) Inc., 375 Hudson Street, New York, New York 10014, USA
Penguin Group (Canada), 90 Eglinton Avenue East, Suite 700, Toronto, Ontario,
Canada M4P 2Y3 (a division of Pearson Penguin Canada Inc.)
Penguin Ireland, 25 St Stephen's Green, Dublin 2, Ireland
(a division of Penguin Books Ltd)
Penguin Group (Australia), 250 Camberwell Road, Camberwell, Victoria 3124, Australia
(a division of Pearson Australia Group Pty Ltd)
Penguin Books India Pvt Ltd, 11 Community Centre, Panchsheel Park,
New Delhi – 110 017, India
Penguin Group (NZ), 67 Apollo Drive, Rosedale, North Shore 0632, New Zealand
(a division of Pearson New Zealand Ltd)
Penguin Books (South Africa) (Pty) Ltd, 24 Sturdee Avenue, Rosebank,
Johannesburg 2196, South Africa

Penguin Books Ltd, Registered Offices: 80 Strand, London WC2R 0RL, England

puffinbooks.com

Published 2008
1

Text copyright © Linda Chapman, 2008
Illustrations copyright © Dawn Apperley, 2008
All rights reserved

The moral right of the author and illustrator has been asserted

Set in Palatino by Palimpsest Book Production Limited,
Grangemouth, Stirlingshire
Made and printed in England by Clays Ltd, St Ives plc

British Library Cataloguing in Publication Data
A CIP catalogue record for this book is available from the British Library

ISBN: 978-0-141-32230-8

lindachapman.co.uk

To Holly and Charlotte Allison

Contents

Chapter One

'Are you ready?' Electra whispered to Splash, her pet dolphin.

Splash nodded, his black eyes sparkling with mischief. 'This is going to be fun!'

'They're coming!' said Electra as she

saw Sasha and Nerissa, two of her mermaid friends, in the distance. 'Quick! Let's get ready to play our trick, Splash!' Her friends were swimming towards them, their silvery-green tails swishing through the water. Nerissa had long brown hair; Sasha's was thick and blonde and fell just past her shoulders.

Electra and Splash dived into a cave. Electra threw an old sheet with eyeholes cut into it over Splash. Then she pulled another one over her own head. It draped down over her, hiding her long red hair and purple seashell bikini.

Splash poked his nose out from under his sheet. 'Hello, hello,' he grinned.

Electra pulled the sheet over his nose. 'Stop it, Splash! You can't be a ghost with a dolphin's nose!'

'I could be a dolphin ghost,' Splash suggested. He opened his mouth and made a bubble come out. 'I could make spooky bubbles.'

'Don't be silly, Splash!' Electra

giggled, pulling the sheet firmly back over his head for the second time. 'Now be quiet. If Sasha and Nerissa hear us it will ruin the trick.'

As their friends got closer, Electra heard Sasha's voice through the water. 'I don't know what Electra was talking about. *I* can't see any rainbow-coloured coral anywhere down here.'

'But she definitely said there was some here,' Nerissa replied.

Electra had to fight the desire to giggle. There weren't really any rainbow-coloured coral; she had just made it up to get Sasha and Nerissa to come to the caves so she and Splash could play their trick on them. Excitement bubbled up inside her. 'Ready?' she whispered to Splash.

'Ready,' he whispered back.

They dived out of the cave together. 'Boo!' they yelled under their sheets.

'Argh!' Sasha and Nerissa shrieked, jumping into each other's arms.

Electra pulled her sheet off. 'It's only us!' she laughed delightedly.

Splash tipped the sheet off his head and caught it in his mouth. 'Tricked you!'

The fear on Nerissa's face turned to relief. 'Electra! Splash! I thought you were ghosts!'

Electra turned a somersault in the water and then, seeing that Sasha was looking quite shaky, she went over and hugged her. 'Are you OK?'

'I was really scared,' said Sasha.

'Did you make up about the coral just to get us here?' Nerissa asked Electra.

Electra grinned. 'Yep. There aren't really any rainbow-coloured coral. I just wanted you to swim past this cave.' She twirled round. 'I love playing tricks!'

'Well, I don't like having them played on me,' said Sasha firmly. 'Come on, Nerissa, let's go.'

But as they turned to go, Nerissa remembered something. 'Oh, Electra. Have you heard the news? My mum and dad are buying a carriage!'

'A carriage!' Electra echoed. Not many of the merpeople who lived around Mermaid Island had carriages.

'It's for my gran really,' Nerissa explained. 'She lives on the other side of the island to us but she's old and can't swim very far now. Mum and Dad have bought it so we can bring her to our house to visit. They're collecting it this afternoon.'

'I'm going round to Nerissa's house tomorrow to see it,' said Sasha. 'I can't wait.'

'I can't wait to *drive* it!' said Nerissa, her brown eyes shining. 'Mum said we're going to have two porpoises to pull it and they're going to have silver harnesses.'

Splash clapped his flippers excitedly.
Porpoises looked very like dolphins
although they weren't nearly so clever.
'Can I come and play with them?'
he said.

'Of course you can,' said Nerissa.

She and Sasha swam off.

Splash swooshed through the water.
'Wow! I can't wait to meet the

porpoises tomorrow. What shall we do today, though, Electra? Shall we go to Turtle Rock?'

Turtle Rock was a large rock that stuck out of the sea to the north of Mermaid Island. There was a large expanse of flat sea around it. Electra and Splash had started going there together to play. Electra would hang on to Splash's fin and they would

whizz through the water together. It was great fun!

'Maybe later,' Electra said. 'But let's play another trick first.' She looked around. 'I think I've got another idea!' The nearby rocks were covered with starfish, green sea kelp and purple seaweed. The seaweed fronds were fringed with little round balls that looked almost like shiny purple sweets. 'We could collect some of these,' Electra said, picking one off the nearest seaweed plant. 'If we wrap them up and put them in a box we can pretend they're sweets.' She tasted one with her tongue. It tasted of salt and old fish. 'They're horrid!' she said, pulling a face. 'It'll be a great trick!'

She started picking the seaweed balls and putting them into the mermaid bag that was slung over her shoulder. 'Come on, Splash! Help me!'

They soon had about thirty of the seaweed balls. 'Let's take them home,' said Electra. She held on to Splash's fin and he swam upwards towards the higher caves where the merpeople lived. Electra kicked her feet. She loved it when Splash pulled her along. She couldn't swim as fast as the other

merchildren because she had been born a human and she had legs and feet, not a tail.

Eight years ago, the merpeople had found Electra all alone in a lifeboat the morning after a terrible storm. She had been only a baby at the time. The merpeople had taken pity on her and given her magic sea powder so she could breathe underwater. Then Maris, a young mermaid, had adopted her.

Electra loved being a mermaid and couldn't imagine living on the land. However, having legs wasn't the only thing that made her different from the other merpeople. Most of them liked living a quiet life, but Electra loved exploring and having adventures. Luckily, Splash liked doing exciting things almost as much as she did!

They reached the cave where they lived with Maris, Electra's mum. There was a curtain of pink shells in the entrance that tinkled in the water currents. In next-door's front garden a tall merman with blonde hair was checking the neat rows of sea cabbages and sea cucumbers growing there. It was Ronan, Sasha's dad.

'Hello, Electra,' he called. 'Your mum's just gone out.'

'That's OK. I wasn't looking for her.' Electra grinned to herself as she thought about the trick she and Splash were about to play.

She and Splash swam in through the curtain of shells to their cave.

'You get a box – there's one in my bedroom that used to have sweets in. I'll get some paper from the craft bag to wrap the seaweed balls up in,' Electra told Splash.

He raced away and came back with a lilac box. There was lots of shiny paper in the craft bag – red, blue and gold. Electra chose the gold and carefully wrapped the seaweed balls up. When she put them in the lilac box on some tissue paper, they looked just like delicious sweets!

Electra placed the lid on the box of pretend sweets. 'OK,' she said, looking at Splash. 'Let's find someone to play our new trick on!'

Chapter Two

Ronan was still in the garden. He had been joined by Sam, Sasha's twin brother. They were raking the sand around the cabbages.

Sam's eyes spotted the box straight away. 'What's that?' he asked.

'Sweets,' Electra said innocently, taking the lid off the box to show what was inside.

Sam swam over. 'Can I have one?'

'I wouldn't mind one myself,' said Ronan, joining him.

Sasha and Nerissa appeared in the doorway of the cave. Sasha's gaze fell on the sweets. 'Oh, wow. Sweets!'

'Have one,' said Electra, holding them out. 'They're really delicious.'

Splash gave a whistle of laughter, which he quickly disguised as a cough.

The others all swam over and each took a sweet from the box.

'They look very tasty,' said Ronan, unwrapping his.

He and the twins and Nerissa

popped the trick sweets into their mouths.

'Yuk!' Sam spluttered.

'Eee!' exclaimed Sasha and Nerissa.

'Urgh!' Ronan spat his out into his hand.

Electra and Splash burst out laughing. 'They're not real sweets!' Electra said gleefully. 'It's a joke!'

'Electra!' Sam exclaimed. 'That's horrid!'

'I really wish you wouldn't play tricks all the time, Electra!' Sasha said crossly.

'My mouth tastes all funny now!' said Nerissa.

But Ronan chuckled. 'It was a clever trick, Electra. Let's go inside and get something to take the taste away.'

They all went into the cave. Ronan took some home-made starfish-shaped biscuits out of a tin. 'Here,' he said, offering them round. 'Not that you deserve any, though,' he said, shaking his head at Electra and Splash. 'Trick sweets! I remember doing that sort of thing when I was younger.'

Electra giggled as she remembered the way he had spat out the sweet. 'I like playing tricks on people.'

'You play way too many of them,' Sasha complained.

'Yeah, they're getting really annoying,' Nerissa put in.

'You do need to be careful with tricks, Electra,' Ronan said warningly. 'If you play too many, people will stop believing anything you say.'

Electra nodded but in her mind she

was already busy planning the next trick. There was all that blue foil in the craft bag and it had given her an idea . . .

After they had finished the biscuits, Electra and Splash swam back to their cave.

'Shall we go to Turtle Rock now?' Splash asked eagerly.

'No. I've thought of another trick.'

Electra went to the craft bag and pulled out a piece of blue foil and a small ball. 'If we put this foil on this ball and stick the ball to a stick then it will look just like a blue-ringed jellyfish. We could hide in the caves and make it pop out at people. I bet it would make them really jump!'

Blue-ringed jellyfish were dangerous jellyfish who loved stinging merpeople. They lived mainly in the deep caves but occasionally they came out near the reef where the merpeople spent their time. Electra didn't mind them too much. Their stings didn't seem to hurt human skin as much as merpeople skin. If she touched them she just got faint itchy marks, but if her friends touched them they got big blue stings that really hurt.

'OK,' Splash agreed. 'But can we go to Turtle Rock after that?'

'Maybe,' Electra said, turning back to the craft bag to start making the pretend jellyfish. She glued the blue foil over the top of the ball so that it fell down around it like a skirt. It looked just like a real jellyfish. The only problem was that the foil-covered ball wouldn't stay on the stick properly. It kept falling off when she waved it about.

'Oh, never mind!' she exclaimed, after it had fallen off for the fifth time. 'It'll do! Come on. Let's go back to the cave. We can hide there and poke it out when someone swims past.'

When they got to the cave, there was no one around. They were just about to swim inside when a small sea horse came bobbing out. He had a curly tail, cheeky dark eyes and two small horns with two pink spots just below them.

'It's Sparkle!' Electra exclaimed.

Sparkle was a young dwarf sea horse who they had met one day in the deepest caves. Most dwarf sea horses were very timid but Sparkle was cheeky and lots of fun. Electra really liked him.

'Hi, Sparkle!' Electra and Splash both called.

Electra held out her hand. The little
sea horse swam on to it, curling his
tail round her finger. She stroked
his head. He rubbed his cheek against
her finger affectionately. 'You are so
cute,' she told him. He bobbed up and
down as if he was nodding and she
grinned. 'We're about to play a trick,'
she told him. 'We're going to pretend

there's a blue-ringed jellyfish and scare people! Look at this, Sparkle.'

She held up the pretend jellyfish on the stick. Sparkle's eyes widened.

'We're going to wave it around like this,' Electra told him.

But as soon as Electra waggled the stick about, the jellyfish ball fell off.

'Oh, bother,' she said crossly.

However, before she could pick it up, Sparkle had dived underneath the skirt of foil that was stuck to the ball. He swam upwards with the ball on his head – Electra couldn't see him because of the foil falling around him. He bobbed through the water and suddenly the ball looked just like a real jellyfish!

He poked his head out and looked at Electra as if saying, *What do you think?*

'That's brilliant!' she said. She turned to Splash. 'It looks so real, doesn't it, Splash?'

He whistled excitedly in agreement.

'Do you want to play the trick with us then, Sparkle?' Electra asked. 'We could use you to make the jellyfish move instead of a stick.' The sea horse gave a huge nod, his eyes glinting mischievously.

Electra grinned. 'Come on then! Let's hide!'

Chapter Three

Electra, Splash and Sparkle went into the cave – Splash squeezed in at the back while Electra and Sparkle floated near the front. The first person to come swimming along was an old, stern-looking mermaid. 'We'd better not jump out at her, she might be cross with us,' Electra whispered to Sparkle. However, the next person to approach the cave was her friend, Hakim.

'Go out now, Sparkle!' Electra hissed.

Sparkle bobbed obediently out of the cave, looking just like a real jellyfish.

'Argh!' Hakim yelled.

Electra and Splash dived out just in time to see Hakim swimming frantically backwards, his arms windmilling wildly.

'There's a jellyfish in the water,

Electra!' Hakim shouted. 'Watch out!'
He fell backwards into an octopus who
was sitting quietly on a rock. The
octopus was not amused and squirted
black ink all over him.

Electra burst out laughing. 'It was a
joke!' she said as Sparkle popped his
head out from under the foil. 'It was
a pretend jellyfish. Look!'

Hakim stared. 'I thought I was going to be stung. I'm glad it wasn't a real one.' He looked down at his ink-stained tail and wiped the ink away from his face. 'Oh, Electra,' he groaned. 'I'm going to be in so much trouble now for getting octopus ink all over me. My mum's going to go mad at me!' Looking rather fed up, he swam on his way.

'Poor Hakim,' Splash said worriedly. 'Maybe we shouldn't play the trick again.'

'Don't be silly!' said Electra. 'It was Hakim's own fault he got ink on his tail – he shouldn't have sat on an octopus.' She turned to Sparkle. 'You were brilliant, Sparkle. Let's do it again.'

The next person to pass by was her schoolteacher, Solon. He was very strict and Electra certainly wasn't going to play a trick on him! But then Sasha and Nerissa came swimming past.

'Let's get them again!' Electra whispered to Sparkle. He nodded

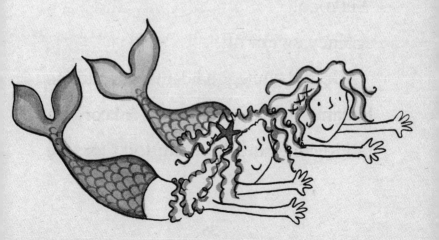

eagerly and, just as they reached the cave, he swam out.

They shrieked.

'Tricked you!' Electra called, swimming out.

They both looked cross.

'It's not funny, Electra,' said Sasha. 'I'm fed up of your tricks!'

'Me too,' said Nerissa, frowning.

'Come on, Nerissa,' Sasha said huffily. 'Let's go!'

They swam off.

Electra shrugged and turned to Sparkle, whose head was once again poking out from under the foil. 'They're such spoilsports,' she said, kissing him on the tip of his nose. 'You were brilliant.'

The sea horse swam on to Electra's shoulder and nuzzled her affectionately.

Splash didn't look too pleased. 'Sasha and Nerissa were a bit cross with us, weren't they? Maybe we should stop now and go and play at Turtle Rock instead.'

'But I want to play the trick again,' said Electra. 'Sparkle does too, don't you, Sparkle?'

Sparkle nodded.

'We can go to Turtle Rock another day,' Electra said to Splash.

'But I want to go there now,' Splash said.

'Well, I'm not going there.' Electra tickled Sparkle with her finger. 'Playing here is *much* more fun!'

Just then Electra spotted two friends from school swimming towards the cave. 'Quick! Hide, you two!' she said.

'Marina and Keri are coming!' Marina and Keri often played tricks themselves and Electra couldn't wait to play one on them.

Electra and Sparkle swam back into the cave but Splash didn't follow them.

'Splash,' Electra said, poking her head out. 'Come on!'

He shook his head. 'I don't want to play any more,' he said huffily.

'Oh, come on!' Electra insisted. 'Don't be so boring!'

Splash swam a little way off. Electra gave up. If he wanted to stay outside the cave he could. He could watch the trick just as well from out there. She dived back inside.

'Ready?' she said to Sparkle.

The sea horse nodded and bobbed out at Marina and Keri when they came swimming past. They shrieked but quickly saw the funny side of the trick.

'I can't believe you managed to fool us with a fake jellyfish!' Marina giggled, grabbing a handful of sea kelp and chucking it at Electra.

Electra grabbed some back and, the next minute, all three mermaids were having a sea-kelp fight, laughing and squealing as the slimy seaweed ran down their backs and hit their faces. Sparkle dodged back into the safety of the cave and watched from there, bobbing up and down.

At last they stopped. Marina and Keri said goodbye and swam on their way, still giggling as they brushed away the remains of the sea kelp.

Sparkle dived under the pretend

jellyfish and swam up with it. 'So you want to play the trick again?' Electra said to him. He nodded.

Electra looked round to find Splash. But there was no sign of him.

Sparkle swam into the cave and looked at Electra as if saying, *Come on!*

Electra hesitated. She wanted to play with Sparkle some more but she felt a bit worried about Splash. Where had he gone? It wasn't like him to go off on his own. Maybe he'd gone home.

'Actually, Sparkle, I'd better not

play with you any more just for now,' she said. 'I should go and find Splash. Do you want to play again tomorrow though?'

Sparkle nodded eagerly. 'OK, I'll see you in the morning,' Electra said to him. 'Let's meet here!'

He waggled his horns and darted away. Electra turned round and began to swim for home. Where was Splash? Where had he gone?

Electra looked and looked but she ended up swimming all the way back to her cave before she finally found

Splash. He was with Sasha and Nerissa in the next-door garden. Electra's friends were draping necklaces of shells round his neck. 'You look beautiful, Splash,' Sasha was saying. She kissed his head.

Electra stared in surprise. What was Splash doing there? Why hadn't he told her he was going home?

Nerissa saw her. 'Hi, Electra! Look at Splash! Doesn't he look cute?'

Electra gave a brief nod. 'Yeah.' She swam towards Splash. 'I've been looking for you.'

Splash looked a bit guilty.

'We've had a great time playing together,' Sasha told Electra.

'You're so lovely, Splash,' Nerissa said, giving him a hug.

Splash nuzzled her arm.

Electra felt a stab of jealousy. 'I'm going inside,' she said.

She swam into her cave. To her surprise, Splash didn't follow her. Her mum was still out and the cave seemed very still and silent. Electra got herself a drink and sat down. It was strange without Splash there to talk to. She twirled a finger in her hair.

A little while later, Splash came swimming in. He went to the kitchen and found a packet of biscuits. He came back into the lounge eating one.

'Thanks for offering *me* a biscuit,' said Electra grumpily.

Splash went back to the kitchen and brought her over a biscuit. He gave it

to her without saying a word and then turned to swim off.

Electra couldn't contain her unhappiness for a single second more. 'What's the matter with you, Splash?' she burst out. 'Why aren't you speaking to me and why did you swim off from the caves like that? I swam around looking for you!'

Splash looked at the floor.

'Well?' Electra demanded when he didn't say anything. 'Why didn't you tell me where you were going?'

'You wouldn't have listened to me anyway,' muttered Splash.

'What do you mean?' Electra said in astonishment.

'You were –' Splash broke off. 'Oh, it doesn't matter,' he said crossly, and he turned his tail on her.

'Splash!' Electra exclaimed. 'Tell me what the matter is.'

But he wouldn't speak.

Frustration flooded through Electra. 'Fine. If you don't want to talk to me then I'm not going to talk to you either!'

She swam angrily into her bedroom and lay down on her bed. She picked up a book but didn't really feel like reading it. Her thoughts just kept going back to Splash. Why was he being so grumpy with her? She hugged her knees to her chest. She didn't know but whatever the reason was, she hoped he'd start speaking to her again soon!

Chapter Four

At supper time, both Electra and Splash hardly said a word.

'Would anyone like any more seaweed salad?' Maris, Electra's mum, asked.

'Yes, please,' Electra muttered. Maris passed it to her.

Silence fell on the table again.

'Please could I have some more cabbage, Maris?' Splash asked quietly.

'Of course.' Maris passed the bowl of sea cabbage along the table.

'Thank you,' Splash said.

There was another silence.

Maris looked from one to the other. 'OK, what's going on?' she asked. 'Usually I can't get a word in edgeways with the pair of you.'

Neither Splash nor Electra said anything.

'Have you had an argument?' Maris asked them.

Electra didn't feel like talking about
it. 'No,' she fibbed.

Splash shook his head.

Maris raised her eyebrows as if she
didn't believe them but to Electra's
relief she didn't press them any further.
'Well, I hope you find your voices
again soon,' was all she said before
changing the subject. 'I saw Nerissa's
family's new carriage this afternoon.'

'What's it like?' asked Electra curiously.

'Very smart,' her mum replied. 'It's made of silver and covered with tiny shells. The two porpoises who pull it are lovely but quite young. They seemed a bit frightened by all the noise at the shops.' She turned to Splash as she got up to clear the plates away. 'I bet they'd like to make friends with

you, Splash. Why don't you go round tomorrow morning and say hello?'

Splash nodded eagerly. 'We could, couldn't we?' he said, seeming to forget about being in a mood and turning to Electra as Maris went through to the kitchen.

Electra felt a rush of relief that he was talking to her again. 'Yeah, but I can't go in the morning,' she said quickly. 'I'm meeting Sparkle.'

The excitement faded from Splash's eyes. 'Oh.'

'We could maybe go in the afternoon, though,' Electra offered.

'It's OK,' Splash muttered. 'I think I'll go on my own in the morning.' He swam quickly away from the table, his face unhappy.

Splash usually slept by Electra's bed but that night he slept in the lounge. Electra missed being able to reach out and touch his head. When she got up, she found her mum in the kitchen but no sign of Splash.

'Where's he gone?' she asked her mum.

'He's gone round to Nerissa's to meet the porpoises,' Maris replied. 'He went out about ten minutes ago. I saw him call round for Sasha.'

Electra ate her breakfast on her own. She wondered what he was doing at Nerissa's and if Sasha and Nerissa were dressing him up in necklaces again. *I think he looks silly wearing necklaces*, she thought.

She set off to meet Sparkle feeling very quiet inside.

The little sea horse was waiting by the cave. He zoomed up and down before landing on her shoulder. 'Hi, Sparkle,' she said in a subdued voice.

Sparkle nudged the pretend jellyfish she was holding.

'Yes, we can play the trick again,' said Electra. But as they swam into the cave she realized that she didn't feel like playing tricks that day. Still, Sparkle seemed keen. He swam under the jellyfish and Electra watched out for people to trick.

They managed to scare Elias from her school, and Nerissa's cousin, Nero.

But although Elias and Nero yelled and jumped and then laughed when they found out it was a trick, Electra just didn't find it as much fun as the day before. It wasn't the same without Splash to laugh with, and she hated knowing that he was off somewhere else in a mood with her.

I miss him, Electra thought. *I really miss him.*

Just then, Sparkle dodged out from under the jellyfish and zoomed into the cave. He looked at her, looked into one of the tunnels that led into the deeper caves and bobbed up and down as if he was trying to tell her something.

'You've got to go back now?' Electra said, trying to understand him.

The little sea horse nodded.

'All right. It was lovely playing with you. I'll see you soon!' Electra said. Sparkle gave her a cheeky look and whizzed away.

Electra swam away from the cave. What should she do next?

As she looked through the water, she spotted a carriage in the distance being pulled by two grey porpoises. A mermaid with long brown hair was driving it. *It's Nerissa*, Electra realized. Sasha was sitting beside Nerissa, and Splash was swimming alongside the carriage. He was swimming very carefully so as not to lose any of the five necklaces that were hanging round his neck.

As Electra watched, Nerissa reined the porpoises in. She had a bit of a

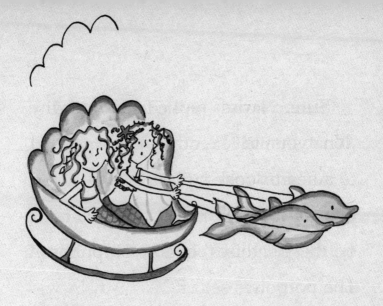

struggle, as they were young and headstrong, and it took her a few moments to get them to obey the tugs on the reins and stop. 'I think I'd better practise starting and stopping,' Electra heard her say rather breathlessly to Sasha.

'Can I have a go at driving then?' Sasha asked.

'Sure,' Nerissa replied. 'Splash, why don't you wait over there?' She pointed to a nearby rock. Splash swam slowly over to it as Nerissa flicked the reins on the porpoises' backs. 'Hup, boys!' The porpoises set off.

Electra glanced over at Splash. He looked a bit bored. Should she go and say hello? She hesitated. *What if he won't speak to me?* she thought. *Oh, I'll try anyway!* she decided.

She had just begun to swim towards him when four blue-ringed jellyfish came swimming out of a nearby cave. Electra gasped and stopped dead.

Blue-ringed jellyfish! Real ones!

The jellyfish floated lazily out into the sea towards where Nerissa was trying to make the porpoises practise stopping and starting. The jellyfishes' dangerous tentacles trailed through the water, their bodies glowing a bright sinister blue.

'Watch out, Nerissa!' Electra yelled, switching direction and swimming past the jellyfish towards her friend's carriage as fast as she could. 'There are jellyfish in the water! Don't come over here!'

Nerissa pulled the porpoises to a

stop as Electra swam up. She frowned. 'We told you we're fed up with your jokes, Electra. We know there aren't *really* jellyfish in the water.'

'Yeah, you're just trying to trick us again,' Sasha said, looking down on her from the carriage seat.

'No, I'm not! LOOK!' Electra yelled, pointing to the blue jellyfish bobbing along in the water behind her.

Nerissa just laughed. 'Electra! That's

just Sparkle pretending to be a jellyfish and you've obviously got some of his friends pretending to be other ones. We're not stupid! Come on, boys,' Nerissa said to the two porpoises. 'Hup!' She flicked the reins. The two porpoises leapt forward past Electra.

'No!' Electra cried in dismay as the carriage headed straight towards the jellyfish. 'Nerissa! STOP!'

The porpoises suddenly caught sight of the jellyfish. Electra could see from the scared looks on their faces that they knew immediately that the jellyfish were real. As the jellyfishes' tentacles

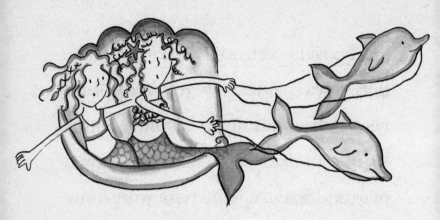

waved towards them the porpoises panicked and tried to swim in opposite directions. The carriage swayed dangerously from side to side.

'Steady,' gasped Nerissa, struggling with the reins as she and Sasha were thrown about on the carriage seat, but the porpoises were too frightened to listen. They pulled the reins out of her hands.

The jellyfish swam closer. The porpoises panicked even more and veered upwards. As they bolted for the surface of the sea, the carriage tipped over and Sasha and Nerissa were flung over the sides. Arms flailing, they tumbled through the water straight towards the stinging jellyfish . . .

Chapter Five

Electra didn't stop to think. Seeing her friends tumbling through the water, she knew she had to help them. She couldn't just watch them be stung. In the blink of an eye, she had dived down among the jellyfish and grabbed

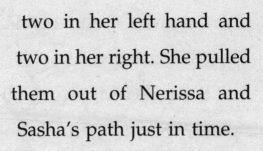

two in her left hand and two in her right. She pulled them out of Nerissa and Sasha's path just in time.

The jellyfish were very surprised and cross to be grabbed. They wrapped their tentacles round her arms and stung her hard, but Electra held on tight. Ignoring the stings, she swam quickly with them to the cave.

Splash was already tipping the necklaces over his head and racing over to her. 'Your hands, Electra! They're hurting you!'

'I'll be OK. Mind out of the way, Splash,' Electra gasped, holding the jellyfish out in front of her. 'I don't want them to sting you!'

She threw the jellyfish into the cave. Looking very relieved to be free again, they bobbed hastily away into the tunnel.

'Ow,' Electra said, looking down at the faint blue marks on her hands, wrists and arms.

'You're hurt,' said Splash, nuzzling her skin in concern.

'It's not too bad.' The stings *did* itch and tingle but Electra felt happy inside. The jellyfish hadn't hurt her anything like as much as they would have hurt Nerissa and Sasha.

'Oh, Electra!' Sasha exclaimed, reaching her. 'You saved us from getting stung. Thank you so much.' From the corner of her eye, Electra saw a look of alarm suddenly cross Splash's face and he shot away through the

water. But before she could call out and ask where he was going, Nerissa hugged her.

'It was so brave of you. Are your hands OK?'

'They hurt a bit,' replied Electra. 'But the stings would have hurt you far more.'

'You're the best friend ever!' Sasha and Nerissa told her.

Electra sighed. 'No, I'm not. I'm sorry I played so many tricks. It was really horrid when I couldn't make you believe the jellyfish were real.'

'We just thought you were joking,'

explained Nerissa. 'But you were so brave just now, we forgive you.'

'Of course we do,' said Sasha. She dived down and grabbed a handful of sea kelp. 'Here,' she said, swimming back with it. 'This will help take the sting away.'

'Thanks.' Electra quickly rubbed the kelp over the blue marks. The horrible tingling feeling faded.

Sasha looked round. 'Where are the porpoises?'

'Oh, no!' exclaimed Nerissa. 'My dad's going to be so mad at me if they get lost or the carriage is damaged.'

The three mermaids stared at each other in alarm.

'Quick!' Electra gasped. 'We'd better go after them!'

The mermaids raced to the surface. *I wonder where Splash went. I wish he was here*, Electra thought as she struggled to keep up with the others. They all burst out of the waves together.

'Look!' Nerissa cried.

Sasha's hands flew to her mouth.

Electra shook the water out of her eyes and stared. The frightened porpoises were racing away across the sea with the carriage bouncing around behind them. Its weight seemed to be making the porpoises panic even more. They were heading straight towards the coral wall that encircled Mermaid Island!

'We've got to stop them!' gasped Electra. 'They're going to crash into the wall!'

'They're too far away. We'll never get to them in time,' wailed Sasha.

'They'll wreck the carriage and hurt themselves!' Nerissa burst into tears.

Electra couldn't just watch. She plunged forward but, as she did so, she saw a dolphin burst out of the water ahead of them. He was racing towards the porpoises, aiming for the gap between the porpoises and the coral wall. 'It's Splash!' Electra cried, stopping.

Splash whizzed through the sea, diving in and out of the waves.

'He's trying to head them off!' gasped Nerissa.

'He's not going to be able to reach them in time,' said Sasha.

'Oh, yes he is!' said Electra. 'Go on, Splash!' she yelled. 'You can do it!'

With a final leap Splash cut in front of the porpoises, diving between them and the wall and blocking their way.

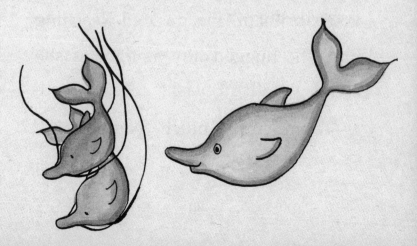

For an awful moment Electra thought they were going to smash into him and hurt him but they swerved to the left.

'He's done it!' she exclaimed as they headed away from the wall.

Splash grabbed the reins in his mouth and pulled the porpoises to a stop.

'Hooray!' cried Nerissa and Sasha.

Splash turned the porpoises round. The mermaids swam to meet him.

'You stopped them! Oh, Splash, you're brilliant!' Electra cried. Reaching him, she hugged him as tight as she could.

'Thank you so much,' Nerissa said,

taking the reins from him and stroking the confused porpoises. 'They could have hurt themselves so badly.'

'I thought I wasn't going to get there in time,' Splash panted.

'I knew you would,' Electra told him. Their eyes met and he touched her arm with his nose.

'You're both so brave,' Sasha said admiringly. Electra and Splash smiled in delight.

'We should take the porpoises back to my dad,' Nerissa said to Sasha. 'I've had enough of carriage driving for today.'

'Me too,' said Sasha. 'Do you want to come?' she asked Electra and Splash.

'No,' Electra said. 'I think we're going to do something else.'

'Not more tricks?' Splash said.

'No more tricks. Not for a long, long time.' Electra grinned. 'But I thought we could go to Turtle Rock – if you still want to?'

'Oh, yes please!' Splash whistled.

'See you later,' Electra called to the others.

'Bye!' they called as they started to lead the porpoises away through the water.

Electra and Splash set off side by side.

'I'm really sorry we argued,' apologized Electra. 'It's been horrible having you not speak to me.'

'I hated it too,' said Splash. 'I'm sorry I was in a mood. I . . .' He looked down. 'I was just feeling jealous of Sparkle.'

'Jealous of Sparkle! Why?' said Electra in astonishment.

'You seemed to be having so much fun with him!' The words burst out of Splash. 'You were playing the trick together and I couldn't join in, and you said it was more fun playing with him than coming to Turtle Rock with me *and* you said I was boring.'

Electra felt awful. 'Oh, Splash, I'm sorry. I didn't mean it. I wasn't really going off with Sparkle. I like him but

he's not you. I was a bit jealous too,' she admitted. 'I didn't like it when you were playing with Sasha and Nerissa.'

'I like them but all they ever want to do is put necklaces on me and then I can only swim slowly. I only went to play with them because I thought you didn't want to play with me,' Splash said.

'We're both silly,' Electra told him. 'We should have just told each other what the matter was. We should never stop speaking again.'

'Never,' Splash agreed. He looked at her anxiously. 'So, am . . . am I

85

still your best friend, Electra?'

'Of course you are,' Electra laughed, putting her arms round him. 'You'll always be my best friend, Splash! Always and forever.'

Splash clapped his flippers in delight. 'Hooray!' he exclaimed, swooshing out from under her arm, leaping into the air and diving perfectly into the water. When he popped back up, his eyes were sparkling. 'Let's race to Turtle Rock, Electra!'

'OK!' Electra took hold of his fin with both hands.

'Are you ready?' he said to her.

She grinned. 'Yes!'

'Then let's go!' Splash said, shooting away like an arrow. Sparkling water sprayed up around them as they whizzed through the waves. Electra felt like she was flying!

'Faster, Splash!' she gasped in delight.

He speeded up and together they raced away across the glittering turquoise sea.

Discover magical new worlds with
Linda Chapman

The Circle of
Secrets & Magic
lindachapman.co.uk

★ **Gallop** with the unicorns at Unicorn Meadows

★ **Fly** with the magical spirits of Stardust Forest

★ **Swim** through Mermaid Falls with Electra and her friends

★ **Play** with new friends at Unicorn School

With great **activities**, gorgeous **downloads**, games galore and an exciting new online fanzine!

What are you waiting for?
The magic begins at

lindachapman.co.uk